Happy First Christmas

Aunt Catherine

Aunt Kelly

Aunt Geni

To Myra

The Christmas Eve Journey

Always be blessed!

Joe Moore

By Joe and Mary Moore

Mary Moore

Published by The North Pole Press

Published by The North Pole Press

Smoky Mountains of Tennessee

ISBN #9781733676137

Cover Design by Mary Moore

Copyright 2019, Joe Moore

Library of Congress Control #9781733676137

Our books may be purchased in bulk for promotional, educational, or business use.
Please contact The North Pole Press by email at sales@thenorthpolepress.com.

Printed in the United States of America

Dedication

For her Christmas wish, a young, very ill girl requested that her father write a poem for her present. In 1822, he presented his daughter with the requested Christmas present. The following year on December 23rd, the poem was published for the first time in New York by the Troy *Sentinel*. It was submitted to the paper by a friend of the author.

The author would not take official credit for the poem until 1837, and it was not until 1855 when Mary C. Moore Ogden would paint "illuminations" for the piece, and its popularity was soon after celebrated throughout the world.

This book is dedicated to Clement Clarke Moore and his genius in bringing one of the greatest joys on earth to light in his poem, "A Visit with St. Nicholas." This Moore (Joe), is honored to bring a revitalization and a new tradition to all those who celebrate Christ's birth and Christmas nearly 200 years after Clement wrote his version.

What is most ironic is that "my" Mary Moore "painted" this version, as Mary Moore-Ogden did Clement's, bringing the poem and its meaning to life as you read it. Are all of us Moores in any way related? Possibly by blood, but most certainly in our love of Christmas, and the jolly old gift-giver who has entertained and given our children (and us) hope and fulfilled our wishes.

So I say thank you to the first Moore family, and hope this version keeps Santa Claus and his wonders alive and meaningful for another 200 years.

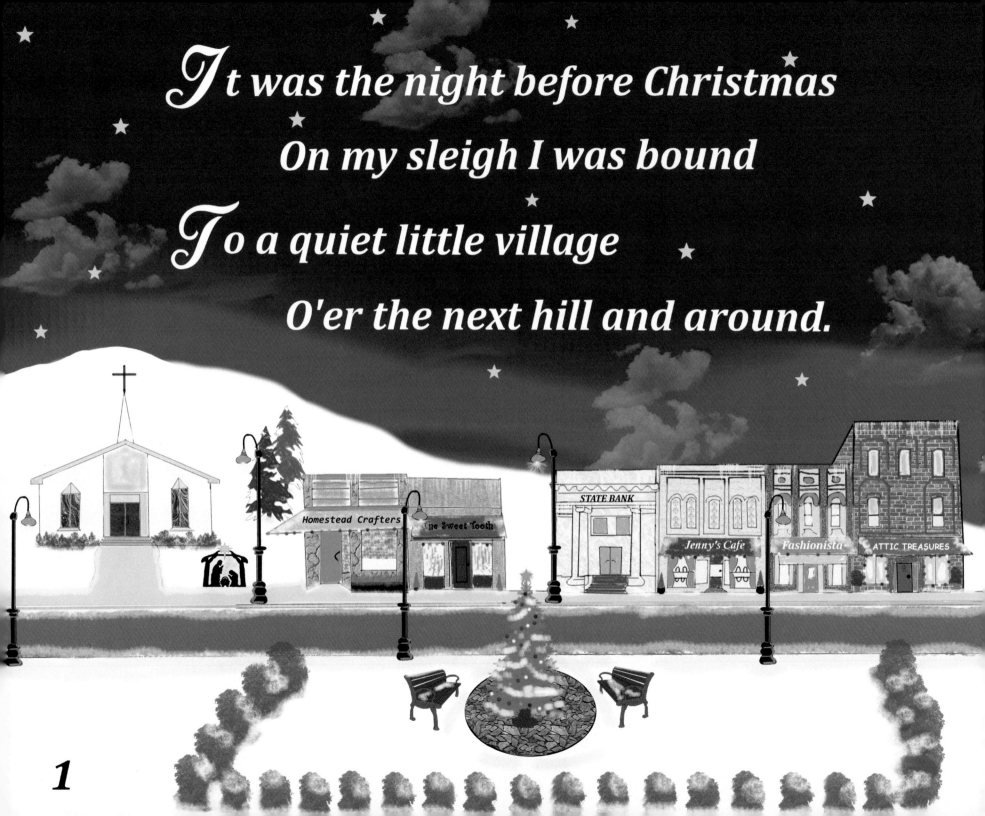

It was the night before Christmas
On my sleigh I was bound
To a quiet little village
O'er the next hill and around.

1

2

I steered my great reindeer
through the clouds and the chill.
Till I saw the house I sought,
The one there on the hill.

3

4

I pulled my team left,
then back to the right.
*A*s we approached the roof,
I pulled the reins tight.

We stopped at the center.

My team checked the length.

For the billionth time they tested

the roof and its strength

8

I heard some commotion
The occupants were stirring!
I could clearly hear footsteps

Even through the wind whirring.

9

I went ahead with my plan,
   it was just Dad that was worried.
*S*o I loaded my pack,
   and down the chimmney I scurried.

When I got to the bottom,
I drew up a big grin,

11

as I looked at the man,
and the shock he was in.

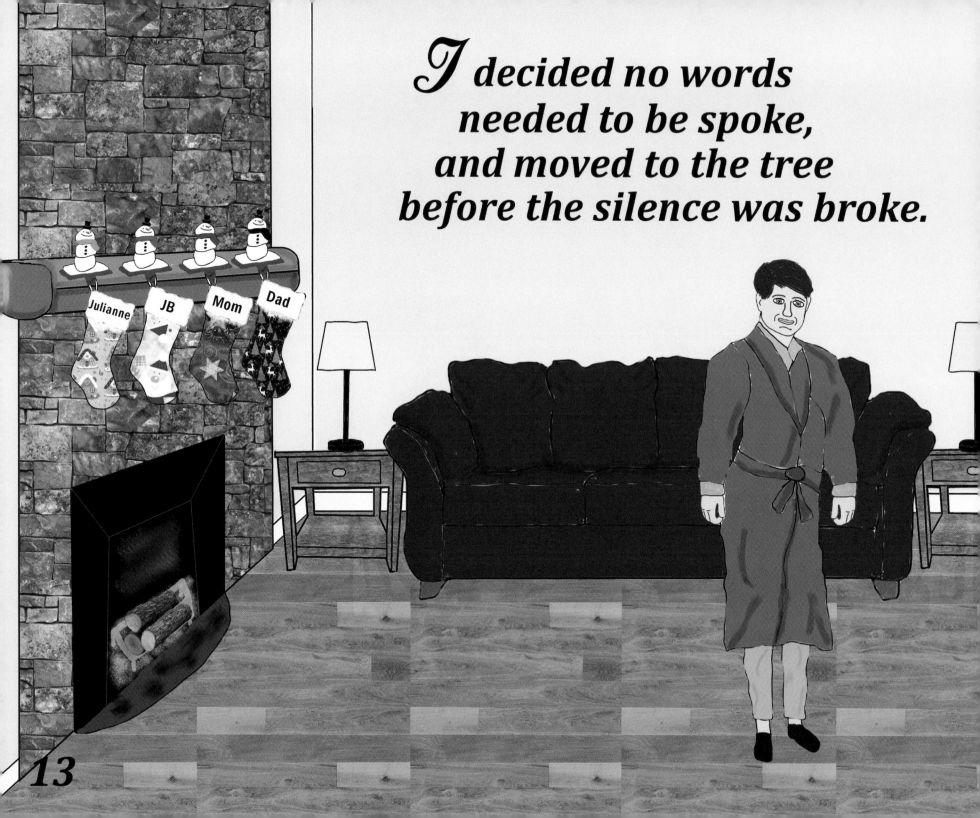

I decided no words
needed to be spoke,
and moved to the tree
before the silence was broke.

13

I opened my bag,
and drew out the packages,
placing them around
like in all the old adages.

14

I reached to the bottom
and finding no more,
I pulled the bag closed
and rose from the floor.

15

I turned to the man
with a wink and a smile
then waited for his question
as was often my style.

16

"Are you really Santa Claus?"
the man finally inquired.
"I am," I said with a grin
he looked puzzled and tired.

17

Then pulled from his reverie
the Dad finally did ask
"Just how and why do you
do your great task?"

18

I had a few moments and was early this night.

19

So taking a cookie and milk
I moved nearer the light.

20

"*I can fly with great haste with my beautiful team. My elves fill my bag until it strains every seam.*

21

Sleigh
Loading
Station

22

I whisk through the towns,
the cities, and lands.
Visiting all the good children,
with my list close at hand.

23

24

As they sleep in their beds
with their happy thoughts,
I reward them with gifts,
and the packages I brought.

25

I bring them presents and loads of fun treats. And place them in stockings and down by the tree.

27

It's a kindness I hope
they'll someday pass on.
And to show love to all
that they come upon.

28

29

God grants me these powers just one night a year.
To remind all the world of His love that's so dear."

30

It was now time to leave
and up the chimney I flew

But I saw the man smile -
and was that a tear, too?

I jumped in my sleigh,
to my team gave a whistle,
*A*nd away we all jetted
with the speed of a missile.

32

33

But I yelled to the man

as I shot from his sight.

"Merry Christmas to all,

and to all a good night. "

About Joe and Mary

Come join Joe and Mary Moore at the North Pole for a while. This author/illustrator team live, work, and play in a world you may know little about. For the last eight years, they have been learning and telling the secrets of the North Pole.

Joe Moore has written numerous novels including the Santa Claus Trilogy, *The Faces of Krampus*, and his delightful children's stories about Santa's helpers, the Santa's Elf Series containing over a half dozen books published with many, many more to come.

Mary Moore has brought Joe's musings to life illustrating all the children's books and *The Faces of Krampus*. She is also the publisher in charge of the North Pole Press and is responsible for making these delightful stories available to you.

Both, Joe and Mary, came from extremely different backgrounds and spent many decades in the business world before living their lives at the top of the world and beyond. Through their books you can learn how Santa accomplishes his miraculous tasks, what each elf does up at the North Pole and their responsibilities to each other and Santa. Who is this Krampus young people are talking about, and what is he to Santa Claus? And you read and see firsthand all the delightful houses and shops of the North Pole that make this land so whimsical and wonderful.

As Tolkien lived in middle earth, Lewis in Narnia, and Rowling in the wizarding world, the Moore's live at the North Pole much of their year. And when they are not there, you can find them in the Eastern United States, mostly at East Tennessee. But it is more fun to visit them through the North Pole.

So enjoy their stories and come to a world only imagined. Come to the North Pole Press.

Joe and Mary love to hear from their fans, you may contact them at joe@thenorthpolepress.com and mary@thenorthpolepress.com

Visit their website www.thenorthpolepress.com and sign up for their newsletters about their new releases, upcoming events and contests.

Santa's Elf Series

Santa's Elf Series© is a series of books to show how everyone works together in the North Pole. It features the diversity of all types of elves and demonstrates how Santa needs everyone to accomplish his miracles. Each book ends with a special message from Santa Claus on how to stay on his famous "Nice List."

Reviews for Santa's Elf Series:

"It is so nice to be able to offer children's books that include a wide diversity of characters, all working together at the North Pole! I think it is very important that a child be able to see characters that reflect their nationality and race in the books that they read."

"The...books have a high rotation even in the spring and summer months! Our parents really appreciate the positive message in each book while kids and parents both love the artwork!"

"Love, love, love the rhyme and beautiful pictures. My children want to read it all the time, and I don't mind [reading] it again and again."

Santa's World, Introducing Santa's Elf Series

The first book in this series explains the genuine reason why Santa brings gifts. It is because he wants to demonstrate God's love, and remind them of the greatest gift of all time. That is, and always has been, the real reason of Christmas. Santa, with the help of the North Pole, developed a series to teach young and old alike about some of his best elves and their responsibilities. The message in this book is about being polite and showing respect.

Color Illustrated 8.5 x 11.5 - Page Count 40
Hardcover ISBN #9780999297742
Softcover ISBN #9780978712907
Ebook   ISBN #9781732378247

Jamie Hardrock, Chief Mining Elf

What if we told you that Santa doesn't bring coal anymore? What if we said there was a much better surprise happening at the North Pole? Our Chief Mining Elf discovered rock candy! Now Santa flies by the naughty children's houses and leaves rock candy for the good children, instead. This endearing tale with beautiful and colorful pictures told in rhyme explains the little-known goings-on at the Hard Rock Candy Mine at the top of the world. The message in this book is about sharing.

Color Illustrated 8.5 x 11.5 - Page Count 36
Hardcover ISBN #9780999297759
Softcover ISBN #9780978712976
Ebook   ISBN #9781732495814

Shelley Wrapitup, Master Design Elf

Beautiful paper, intricate bows, whimsical gift tags, colorful ribbons, all are the work of one of Santa's most creative elves, Shelley Wrapitup. Just as her name suggests, she wraps all the presents and puts the tags on good and tight, so Santa knows just where they go. Through colorful illustrations, rhyme, and alluring details, Shelley's book teaches your child to read in a fun and engaging way. And even though Shelley can make a huge mess, she always cleans up after herself. And that is the message from Santa to your child at the end of Shelley's story.

Color Illustrated 8.5 x 11.5 - Page Count 34
Hardcover ISBN #9780999297766
Softcover ISBN #9780978712983
Ebook   ISBN #9781732495821

Keeney Eagleye, Naughty/Nice List Manager

What if I told you hundreds of thousands of elves came and went to the North Pole every night? Add to this, one of Santa Claus' most important elves was keeping an eye on who is naughty and nice all year long. Keeney is the one that the elves meet at night, as they fly up in their jet packs. With rhyme, stunning pictures, and a charming story, this book teaches children to behave whether at home, school, or with their friends. Santa's message in this book is to always say your prayers and give your worries to God.

Color Illustrated 8.5 x 11.5 - Page Count 34
Hardcover ISBN #9780999297773
Softcover ISBN #9780978712945
Ebook   ISBN #9781732495807

Sarah Buttons, Master Doll Maker

Cuddly animals and action figures and baby dolls, oh my! Where would Santa be if he didn't have tons of these at Christmas? Well, thankfully because of Sarah Buttons, he need not concern himself with that problem. With lyrical rhymes, adorable pictures, and a delightful storyline, Sarah is a favorite tale of for many families.

Santa's message is that we should always be grateful for everything in our lives. It is reasonable and proper to desire more in life, but we should never forget to give thanks for what we already have.

Color Illustrated 8.5 x 11.5 - Page Count 34
Hardcover ISBN #9780999297780
Softcover ISBN #9780978712969
Ebook   ISBN #9781732378292

Ford MacHarley, Master Wheelsmith

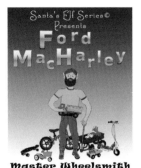

"Award Finalist in the Children's Fiction (Ages 3-6) category of the 2018 American Fiction Awards"

Cars, trucks, bicycles, tricycles, wagons, scooters...what do they have in common? They all have wheels! And Ford MacHarley is our Master Wheelsmith. So whether Santa needs a remote control car or a new bicycle, he counts on Ford to get what he needs.

Santa's message is about bullying. Don't do it, and don't be subjected to it. Santa takes a firm stance on this behavior.

Color Illustrated 8.5 x 11.5 - Page Count 32

Hardcover ISBN #9780999297797

Softcover ISBN #9780999297711

Ebook   ISBN #9780999297797

Carol Joynote, Chief Music Coordinator

Releasing in late summer of 2019, Carol is the seventh book in the series. She is in charge of all the beautiful music of the North Pole. Whether a big brass band, a stunning choir, or carolers wandering the North Pole, Carol oversees all the musical activities to make certain everyone stays in their holiday good mood.

Santa's message is about diversity and acceptance.

Color Illustrated 8.5 x 11.5

Hardcover ISBN #9781733676151

Softcover ISBN #9781733676168

Ebook   ISBN #9781733676175

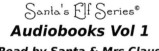

Audiobooks Vol 1
Read by Santa & Mrs Claus
All 3 Books Included

Santa's Elf Series © Vol 1

Audiobook ISBN #9781733676113

Audiobooks Vol 2
Read by Santa & Mrs Claus
All 3 Books Included

Santa's Elf Series © Vol 2

Audiobook ISBN #9781733676120

CPSIA information can be obtained at www.ICGtesting.com
Printed in the USA
LVIW012010051119
636480LV00001B/2